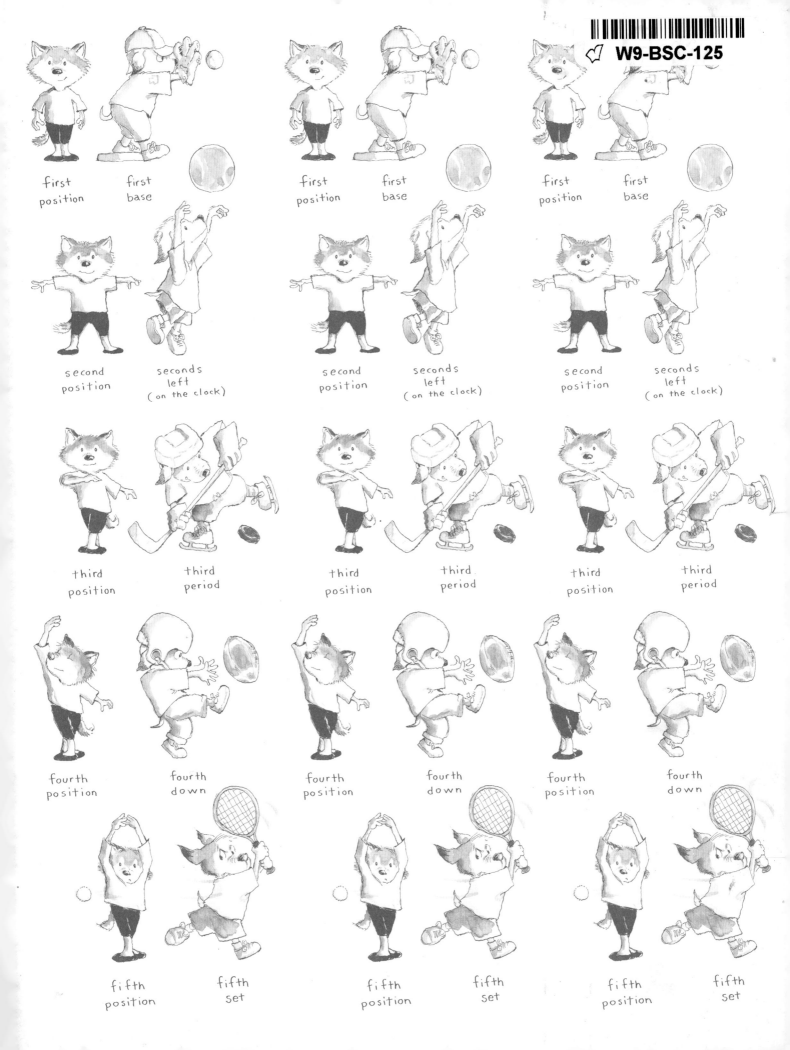

first
position

first
base

second
position

seconds
left
(on the clock)

third
position

third
period

fourth
position

fourth
down

fifth
position

fifth
set

Ballerino Nate

Kimberly Brubaker Bradley
pictures by R. W. Alley

Dial Books for Young Readers

DIAL BOOKS FOR YOUNG READERS
A division of Penguin Young Readers Group
Published by The Penguin Group
Penguin Group (USA) Inc., 375 Hudson Street, New York, NY 10014, U.S.A.

Penguin Group (Canada), 90 Eglinton Avenue East, Suite 700, Toronto, Ontario, Canada M4P 2Y3
(a division of Pearson Penguin Canada Inc.)
Penguin Books Ltd, 80 Strand, London WC2R 0RL, England
Penguin Ireland, 25 St. Stephen's Green, Dublin 2, Ireland (a division of Penguin Books Ltd)
Penguin Group (Australia), 250 Camberwell Road, Camberwell, Victoria 3124, Australia
(a division of Pearson Australia Group Pty Ltd)
Penguin Books India Pvt Ltd, 11 Community Centre, Panchsheel Park, New Delhi - 110 017, India
Penguin Group (NZ), Cnr Airborne and Rosedale Roads, Albany, Auckland 1310, New Zealand
(a division of Pearson New Zealand Ltd)
Penguin Books (South Africa) (Pty) Ltd, 24 Sturdee Avenue, Rosebank, Johannesburg 2196, South Africa
Penguin Books Ltd, Registered Offices: 80 Strand, London WC2R 0RL, England

The publisher does not have any control over and does not assume
any responsibility for author or third-party websites or their content.

Library of Congress Cataloging-in-Publication Data
Bradley, Kimberly Brubaker.
Ballerino Nate / Kimberly Brubaker Bradley ; illustrated by R.W. Alley.
p. cm.
Summary: After seeing a ballet performance, Nate decides he wants to learn ballet, but
he has doubts when his brother, Ben, tells him that only girls can be ballerinas.
ISBN 0-8037-2954-5
[1. Ballet dancing—Fiction. 2. Dogs—Fiction.] I. Alley, R. W., ill. II. Title.
PZ7.B7247Bal 2006 [E]—dc22 2004017822

The art was done in pen and ink, watercolor, and a few colored pencils on Strathmore Bristol.

On the first day of the last week of kindergarten, Nate brought home a permission slip. "We're going to a ballet," he said.

"Yuck," said Nate's brother, Ben. "We're going too. Yuck, yuck, triple yuck." Ben was in second grade. He knew almost everything.

"What's a ballet?" Nate asked.

"Stupid stuff," said Ben. "Girls in dresses."

Mom said, "That's not true, Ben. Ballet is a type of dancing. It's very beautiful. Sometimes ballets even tell stories." She looked at Nate's permission slip. "This ballet is called *The Springtime Garden*."

"Sarah from my class is dancing in it," Ben said. "Yuck."

"Please stop saying 'yuck,'" said Mom.

Nate loved the ballet. He loved the fluttery costumes that the dancers wore. He loved the way the dancers jumped and leaped and spun. He loved the way their movements looked like music.

"I want to learn ballet," Nate said when he got home.

"You *can't,*" Ben said. "You're a boy."

"But I want to," Nate said. "Can I, Mom, can I, please?"

"Classes don't start in the summer," Mom said. "But maybe in the fall.
I'll find out how old you have to be."

All summer Nate danced. He danced on the smooth cold tile in the kitchen. He danced in the long tickly grass on the lawn.

He danced on the rough hot driveway.

Mom read him books about ballet. Nate learned the words *ballerina,* and *plié,* and *tutu.*

"Boys don't dance," said Ben.

"Yes, I do," said Nate. "Watch!" He jumped into the air and spun around, and came down on his toes like a real ballerina.

Just before school started again, Mom said, "Good news, Nate! I talked to Miss Nadia from the ballet school. She says you can join the new beginner class."

"Yeah!" Nate cheered. "I get to be a ballerina!"

Ben laughed. "Boys can't be ballerinas!"

"Yes, they can," said Nate.

"No, they can't," said Ben.

He said it again at night when they were supposed to be asleep. "Boys can't be ballerinas. They never, ever, ever can."

Ben knew almost everything. Nate chewed the inside of his lip. What if Ben was right?

"One thing I know about ballerinas," Ben said in the morning. "They all have to wear pink shoes."

Nate was horrified. "I can't wear pink shoes!"

"You'll have to," Ben said. "Pink shoes and a dress."

Nate hated shoes. He hated pink. He hated dresses. All summer long he had danced in bare feet and shorts.

He started to cry.

Dad came in. "What's the matter, Nate?"

"Ballet shoes are pink!"
Nate wailed.

"Not always," Dad said.
"They make black ballet
shoes and white ones."

"And I don't want
to wear a dress!"
sobbed Nate.

"You won't have to," said Dad.
"Why did you think so?" He
looked at Ben. "Ben?"

"All ballerinas wear pink shoes
and dresses," said Ben.

"That's not true," said Dad.
"I promise."

"And all ballerinas are girls," said Ben.

"Most ballerinas are girls," said Dad. "Not all. Nate, tell me, how many girls played on Ben's Little League team?"

"Two," said Nate. He sniffed.

"So most of Ben's Little League team was boys," said Dad. "Can girls play Little League?"

"Yes," said Nate. He felt a little better.

"In Little League the girls wore the same uniforms as the boys," Ben said.

Nate hid his head in his arms.

On Monday they went to the ballet school. Inside the hallway, two big girls were stretching on the floor. They wore pink tights and shiny pink shoes. "Girls," said Ben.

"I don't care," said Nate. But he did.

They heard music coming from a classroom. Nate looked inside.

Three more big girls were doing exercises. Nate smiled.

Ben said, "They're *all* girls."

"Ben, please go wait for me in the lobby," said Mom.

At the next doorway, Mom said, "Nate, I think this is your class."
Nate peeked in. There were five little girls inside. "Go on," said Mom.

Nate loved the ballet teacher. He loved the ballet class.

But on the way home Ben said, "Was I right?"
and Nate miserably nodded.

"See?" said Ben. "All ballerinas are girls."

"They're not," said Mom.

Nate said, "They were."

Friday Mom said she had a surprise for Nate. "I'm going to take you to a real ballet."

"Our school trip was to a real ballet," Ben said. "Sarah was a petunia."

"Yes," Mom said. "That was a real *ballet-school* ballet. This is a professional one. The dancers Nate and I will see get paid to dance. Dancing is their job."

"Like professional baseball players," Dad said. "Major-league dancing. Have fun."

The theater was much bigger and fancier
than the one Nate's school had gone to. The
stage was enormous.

The curtain went up. Nate held his breath. The lights grew brighter, and the people on the stage began to dance. They were amazing! Watching them made Nate's feet want to dance. Dancers lifted other dancers high into the air. They looked as if they were flying.

"They're beautiful!" Nate said.

He had been watching the dance so hard, he hadn't noticed the dancers. Now he did. "They're boys," he whispered. "Half of them are boys."

"Men," said Mom. "Yes. They are."

When the ballet was finished, Mom took Nate to a door at the side of the theater, and after a while one of the dancers came out. He smiled at Nate.

"Are you a ballerina?" Nate asked.

The dancer shook his head. "No," he said, "I'm not. Only the very top dancers in a company are called ballerinas. And anyway, men can't be ballerinas."

Nate looked at the ground. He felt like crying. "I know," he said. "That's what my brother told me."

The man lifted Nate's chin.
"Men can't be ballerinas, because
the word *ballerina* means
'woman dancer,'" he said.
"I just call myself a dancer.
But if I wanted to use a
word like ballerina, I'd
say *ballerino*. Ballerino
is the word for men."

"Oh," said Nate.
"Are you a ballerino?"
"Not yet," said the
man, "but I dance."
"Oh," said Nate.
"Oh, so do I!"

He
couldn't
wait to
tell Ben.

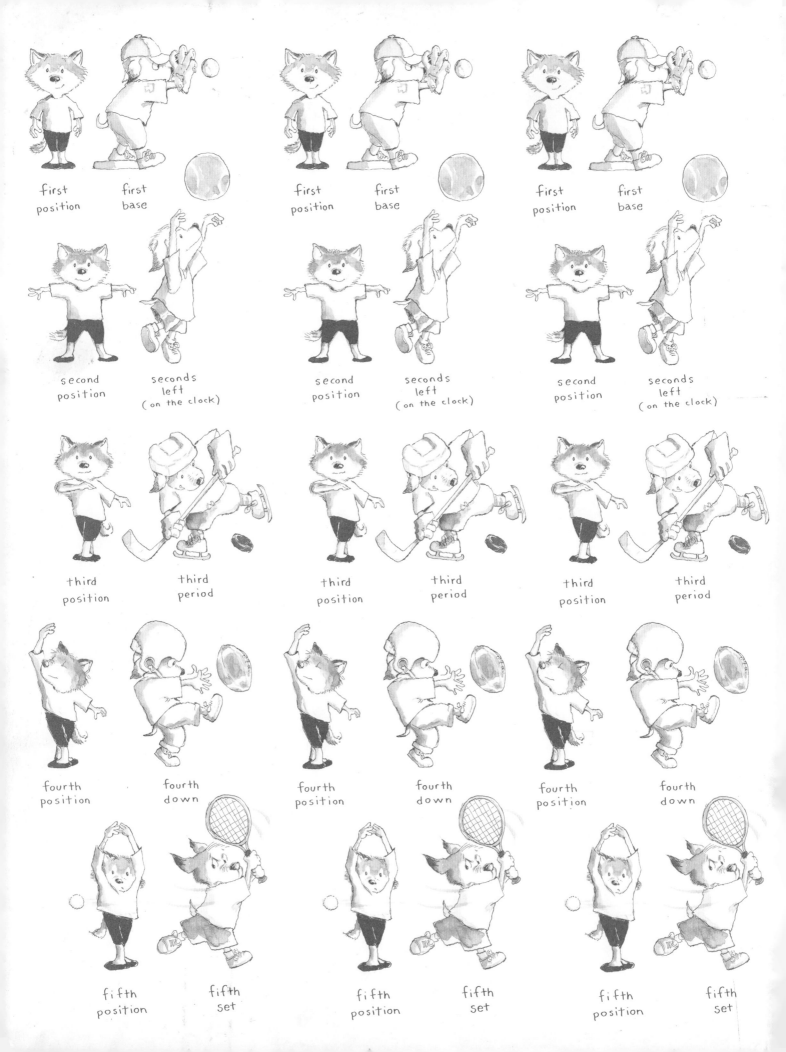

first
position

first
base

second
position

seconds
left
(on the clock)

third
position

third
period

fourth
position

fourth
down

fifth
position

fifth
set